Amis and Amiloun

translated by Edith Rickert

Amis and Amiloun

Table of Contents

Amis and Amiloun..1
    translated by Edith Rickert..1

Amis and Amiloun

translated by Edith Rickert

Kessinger Publishing reprints thousands of hard-to-find books!

Visit us at http://www.kessinger.net

For love of God in Trinity,
All that be gentle, hark to me,
Par amour, I you pray:
What whilom fell beyond the sea,
Of two barons of great bounty,
Men of honour were they.

Their fathers both were barons bold,
Town and tower for to hold,
Of high kin, I you say.

To hearken of these children two,
How they were, in weal and woe,
It is dolour, i' fay.

Listen now, and ye shall hear in what land they were born, and what they were called, and how they were nought akin, and how they were good and kind, and came to be friends, and were sworn brethren; and how they were dubbed knights, and how they fared in weal and woe.

In Lombardy, as I understand, there dwelled long ago two noble barons with their ladies, and each had a son. Now these knave children, who were afterwards so doughty and so true that Jesus rewarded them, were born on the same night; and the one was called Sir Amis in his christening at the church, and the other Sir Amiloun. They throve wondrously, and were so fair and courteous, brave and good, that when they were five years old all their kin were blithe of them, and when they were seven all men had joy to behold them, and when they were twelve winters old they were the fairest of bone and

Amis and Amiloun

blood in all that land.

In that time the Duke of Lombardy let send his messengers for earls and barons, free and bond, and ladies bright in bower, to come to a rich feast that he was making with great mirth, in honour of Jesus Christ our Saviour, and so on that day he gathered much folk together.

Then these two bold barons came to court with their sons, and when young and old were assembled the lords beheld how fair these children were of body, and how much alike to look upon, and how wise of lore; and all said in truth that never were such bairns as these born in the world. And they were so like in looks and stature that there was no man at court, earl, baron, swain or knight, poor or rich—not even their own father and mother—that could tell them apart save by the colour of their clothes.

The rich duke held his feast, with earls and bold barons, for a fortnight, with meat and drink as merry as might be, to gladden folk and make them blithe; and they had all manner of melody to show the craft of each minstrel. And on the fifteenth day they thanked the duke and took their leave to go home.

But he called the two noble barons aside, and prayed them as his friends to remain at court, and let their two sons be in his service; and he said that he would dub them knights and look to their finding ever more, and keep them as lordings of high lineage.

The barons and their ladies answered at once that they were fain to have their dear sons in his service, and gave the children their blessing, and besought Jesus, King of Heaven, to shield them from care; and often they thanked the duke, and so went home to their own countries. 4 Thus were child Amis and child Amiloun nurtured at court, and rode a-hunting under the wood-boughs; and they came to be known over all the land as the worthiest that might be. So well they loved each other as never children did before; and no love bred in blood and bone might be truer than was theirs.

On a day they plighted troth together that never as long as they might live or stand, by day and night, in weal and woe, for right or wrong, would they fail to hold together in every need, in will and word and work. Wherever they might be in the land, from that day forward, neither would fail the other; and thereto they held up their hands. 5 Now the duke was glad to have these two children riding seemly by his side, for they were lief and

Amis and Amiloun

dear to him; and when they were fifteen winters old, he dubbed them both knights, and found them, as they had need, in horses and weapons and splendid raiment, as princes proud in pride. He loved them so that he gave them whatso they would of white steeds and brown, and in whatsoever place they went all the land spake of them, alike in tower and town; and whenever they went into joust or tournament, they were known as the doughtiest that rode with shield and spear. Even more, he esteemed them so well for their worth and wisdom and bounty, that he set them both in great office, making Sir Amis his chief butler, and Sir Amiloun chief steward in the hall to govern his men. In this service they spared not to get a good name, and wrought so well with their riches and power that all who knew them loved them for their blithe bearing; and the duke himself cherished them most of any men alive.

Now this duke had a chief steward in charge of all his land, a doughty knight himself, who ever tried to bring them to shame through guile and treachery; for he hated and envied them in that they were so good and gentle, and in that the duke was so well their friend; and often he spoke to his lord about them with bitter and false words.

Within two years from this time, a messenger came to Sir Amiloun, and said how by God's will death had taken both his father and mother; and then was he right sorrowful, and went to the duke and did him to understand the case, and how he must go home to be seised of his land.

The duke answered him in courteous wise, saying: "So God speed me, Sir Amiloun, since thou must go, I am more grieved than ever before when any friend left my court. And if at any time it chance that thou art in war or other distress, and hast need of my help, come or send thy messenger, and with all the power of my land I will avenge thy wrong!"

But Sir Amiloun was more deeply sorrowful to part from Sir Amis, and thought only of him. He went to a goldsmith, and bade him make two cups of an equal weight and size, and as like as their two selves; 7 and they were so richly wrought that he paid for them three hundred pounds.

When Sir Amiloun was all ready to fare on his journey, Sir Amis was so full of grief that he all but swooned away and going to the duke in his trouble, he prayed him fair "Sir, for charity's sake, give me leave also to depart. Unless I may go with my brother, my heart will break in three!"

Amis and Amiloun

But the duke answered at once, albeit kindly: "Sir Amis, my good friend, would ye both leave me now? Certes, nay! Were ye both gone, then would my joy depart with you and my sorrow awaken! Thy brother must home to his own lands; wend thou a little with him on his journey, but come back again to-day."

When they had busked them ready for to ride, all that day they made great mourning, these doughty knights; and when they came out into the plain, and the moment arrived for them to part, they dismounted from their horses, and when they were both afoot, said Sir Amiloun, who was wise in counsel: "Brother, as we are troth-plight from this day forward never more to fail each other in weal or woe, but to help in time of need, be now true to me as I shall be true to thee, God help me! And, brother, I warn thee now, for love of Him that bare the crown of thorns to save all mankind, be never forsworn against thy lord; for if thou art, thou shalt be lost ever more without end. Ever hold thy troth and never do treason; and remember me, Amiloun, now that we must part asunder.

And, brother, I forbid thee the fellowship of the false steward, for certes, he will do thee hurt!"

As they stood so, these brethren bold, Sir Amiloun drew forth the two golden cups, alike in all ways, and bade Sir Amis choose which he would have, saying: "My dear brother, each of us shall keep one: for the love of God, let it never be taken from thee, but remember me when thou dost look upon it; it is a token of our parting!"

Thereupon, with weeping and great sorrow they kissed and commended each the other to the King of Heaven, sprang on their steeds, and went their several ways.

Sir Amiloun returned to his castle, and was seised in the land of his forefathers; and then he espoused a lady bright in bower, and brought her home with great honour and solemnity.

Let us leave him now with his wife in his own land—God prosper them!—and tell of Sir Amis, how, when he came again to court, all were blithe to see him and blessed him, save only the steward who aye through envy and hatred strove to bring him into care.

On a day it befell that they two met, and the steward greeted him fair, saying: "Sir Amis, thou art full sorrowful that thy brother is gone away from thee, and certes, so am I! But I

Amis and Amiloun

counsel thee to think no more of his wending, and let be thy mourning; if thou wilt be kind to me, I will be to thee a better friend than ever he was yet. Sir Amis," he said, "by my rede, we shall swear brotherhood and plight our troths. Be true to me, in word and deed, and I shall, God help me, be as true to thee!"

Sir Amis answered: "I gave my word to the gentle knight, Sir Amiloun, though he be gone from me, that whiles I may go or speak, I shall not break my troth for weal or woe. For by the faith that God gave me, I have found him so good and kind since first I knew him, that as we are now bound to each other, whereso he wanders in the world I shall be true to him; for an I were forsworn, then were I lost, and bitterly it should me rue! Get me friends whereso I may, I shall never change him for another!"

Thereupon the steward was fierce of temper, and went near mad for wrath, and swore by Him that died on the Rood: "Thou traitor, unkind of blood, this nay shall cost thee dear! I warn thee now that I shall be thy strong foeman ever after!"

Sir Amis answered: "Sir, I care not a straw for that! Do all thou canst!"

So began the trouble. The two barons parted in wrath, and the steward never ceased trying to undo that doughty man. But thus they were together at court well half a year and longer, before, with guile and treason, he was able to work him woe.

Now in the summer-time, as we tell in story, the duke made a feast whereto was gathered much seemly folk, earls and barons of all degrees, and proud ladies; and there was great banqueting and merriment in his palace. And there was the duke's young daughter, Belisaunt, fifteen winters old, who was accounted the fairest to look upon in all that land.

She was there with her ladies and maidens bright in bower, and attended with all honour and solemnity.

Fourteen nights the feast lasted, of barons and gay brides, gentle knights and serjeants to wait in hall; but the butler, Sir Amis, was held throughout to be the flower among them, alike the bravest and the comeliest. And when the guests were all departed, that merry maid asked each one of her women: "So God help you, who was held for the doughtiest knight, and the seemliest and the fairest in all the land?"

Amis and Amiloun

Her maidens answered: "Madam, by St. Saviour, we shall tell thee the truth the fairest man and most honoured of earls, barons, knights and swains, is Sir Amis, the duke's butler—his peer is not in the world!"

And when they had so spoken, all her love fell on that gentle knight, yet so that no man knew of it. Whenever she saw him ride or go, she thought her heart would break in twain, for that she might not speak with him; and she wept many a time and dwelled in such care and sorrow, by night and by day, that she fell sick. Her mother came to her and began to ask of her trouble, seeking to give help; but she said only, her pains were so sharp that she would soon lie buried in the clay.

One morning, the rich duke and many proud princes and lords busked them to hunt the deer; but Sir Amis, for a malady that he had, stayed at home; and when the lordings were gone with their huntsmen and bent bows to hunt in the hoar woods, he bethought him that he would walk in the garden to solace him a little; and there he was soon content, as he lay under a bough, to hear the birds singing.

Now as the duke's daughter lay sick in her bed, her mother entered with doleful countenance, and all the ladies came also to comfort her.

"Arise," she said, "daughter mine, and go out into the garden, this seemly summer's day, and when thou hearest the birds singing joyfully, thine own care shall depart!"

Then that sweet maiden arose, and with her ladies walked in the garden, where, that bright summer's day, the sun was shining with seemly rays of light. She heard the sweet notes of the nightingale singing merrily on the tree; but her heart was so sore beset with love-longing, that no music might gladden her. As she walked in the orchard to lighten her care, she beheld Sir Amis where he lay under a bough, the better to hear the glee of the birds.

When she saw him there, she was so glad that she could not tell her joy, and she thought to herself that nothing should keep her from revealing all her state. So she went up to him, that sweet maiden, and thought that not for all this world's goods would she forbear to speak with him. And as soon as the gentle knight saw her coming towards him, he arose and went to meet her and saluted her courteously with goodly words.

Amis and Amiloun

Anon the merry maiden bade her women to withdraw them hence, and when they two were alone together, she bemoaned her to Sir Amis, saying: "Sir Knight, all my heart is set on thee, and I can think of nothing else, night and day! Unless thou wilt love me again, my heart will break in three, and I may not live longer! Thou art a gentle knight, and I am a gay bride in bower, of high lineage, and so do I love thee all the while that my joy is forlorn! Plight me thy troth to be true, and to change me for no other that is born in this world; and I will plight thee mine, never to be forsworn till God and death do part us!"

The gentle knight stood still, and all his mood changed as he considered, but he said in courteous wise: "Madam, as thou art come of noble blood and shalt be heir of this land, bethink thee, for His sake that died on the Rood, of thine own honour! King's son or emperor is not too good for thee; and certes, it were wrong to set thy heart on a knight that hath neither land nor other possessions. If we should once begin that game, and any of thy kindred knew of it, we should soon lose all our joy in this world, for the sin would move God presently to wrath. If I should put such shame upon my lord, then were I an evil traitor, and certes, it may not be! Dear madam, take counsel of me, and think what would come of this—verily, nothing but woe!"

Then that merry maiden answered: "Sir Knight, thy crown is not shaven! By God that bought thee dear, art thou priest or parson, monk or canon, that thou shouldst preach to me? Thou art not fit to be a knight going among fair maidens! Rather shouldst thou have been a friar! He that learned thee so to preach—the devil take him, though he were my brother! But," she said, "by our Maker, all thy preaching helps nought, stand thou never so long! Unless thou grant me thy will, my love shall be dearly avenged with hard and fierce pains. I will tear my clothes and my kerchief and say thou didst use thy strength to wrong me; and by the law of the land thou shalt be taken and doomed to hang on high!"

The gentle knight stood still, troubled at heart, and spake no word, but only thought: "Except I grant her will, she will ruin me with her speech ere I can get away; and if I do my lord this wrong, I shall be drawn by wild horses." He was loth to deceive the duke, but well more sorry to lose his life. In the end, he thought it better to grant what she asked than to die, and he said to her: "For the love of God, King of Heaven, listen to me. As thou art a maiden good and leal, bethink thee how often we should bitterly repent this deed, and let us wait a sevennight, and then, as I am a true man, I will grant thee thy will!"

Amis and Amiloun

But that gay maiden answered and swore by Jesu: " Thou 'scapest not so away! Thou shalt plight troth with me now, as thou art a true and gentle knight, to keep that day."

Thereto he assented, and they plighted troth and kissed; and she passed again into her chamber, so glad and fain that to none could she tell her joy.

Sir Amis then went into the hall to await his lord's coming; and when the duke had returned from the deer-hunt, with his great nobles, he asked anon after his daughter, and he was told that she was merry again, and her sorrow was away. They brought her to dine in the hall that day, and rejoiced, and thanked God for her sake.

When the lords were set on the dais with their sweet ladies, they were served at meat full richly, as proud princes with mirth and state; and the maiden, where she sat among her women, cast her eyes an hundred times on Sir Amis, and would not look away. And all the while, the treacherous steward spied upon them fast till he wist all that she did; and by the look of her, he perceived that great love was betwixt those two, and he was sore aggrieved, and thought in a little time to beguile them and bring them into care. Thus this merry maid ate in the hall, four days or five, and as soon as ever she saw Sir Amis, all her trouble was gone and she was glad of her life. Whether he sat or stood, she watched him ever; and the steward, with bitter wrath, presently brought them both into mischief and sorrow—accursed may he be! Another day, when the duke with his meiny was gone deer-hunting, the merry maid, Belisaunt, went to the chamber where Sir Amis was, knowing well the way thither; and the steward lurked in another room there beside, and when he saw her gliding along, ran quickly after, to spy upon them both.

When the maiden found Sir Amis alone, she said: "Hail, Sir Amis, to-day a sevennight is passed since we plighted our troth; therefore I am come to know whether thou wilt forsake me, or, as thou art courteous and holden to be a gentle knight, thou wilt take me truly as thou didst promise?"

"Madam," said he, "I would fain espouse thee and hold thee for my wife; but if thy father heard it said that I had wronged his daughter, he would drive me out of his land! If I were the king of this country and had more goods to my hand than any other five, gladly would I spouse thee, but, certes, I am a poor man—woe is me!"

Amis and Amiloun

"Sir Knight," answered the maiden gently, "for love of St. Thomas of India, why wilt thou ever say me nay? Though thou be never so poor, I may find thee riches enow!"

Then he bethought him, and took that merry maid in his arms and kissed her and made her his own. And all the while the steward was close to the wall to hearken, and through a little hole he watched them as they sat there together, until presently he was fiercely wroth, and strode away as he were mad, to reveal her secret.

As soon as the duke came home, the steward went to meet him, and began to unravel what be knew: "My lord duke, by St. John, I must warn thee of the harm that hath come to thee. There is a thief in thy court, though it grieves my heart and I am ashamed to say it; for certes, he is a treacherous villain that hath stolen upon thy daughter!"

The duke was deeply enangered and cried: "Who hath done me that shame? Tell me, I prithee!"

"Sir," said the steward, "by St. James, I can tell thee right well, and mayest thou hang him to-day! It is Sir Amis, thy butler, who hath ever been false, and now hath undone thy daughter, as I myself saw, and will prove before them both so that they cannot gainsay me!"

Then was the duke wild with rage, and ran into the hall like one mad, and with a sharp falchion struck at his butler standing there, but missed him.

Sir Amis was afraid, and ran into a chamber and shut the door between them, to hide his head; and the duke struck after him such a dint that the falchion went through the door. All that stood about the duke besought him to slake his anger; but he swore by Christ that he would not, for all the wealth of this world, unless that traitor were slain! "I have done him great honour, and now the vile wretch hath wronged my child! Not for all the joy of this world, would I give over to slay him with my two hands!"

"Sir," quoth Sir Amis, "first let thine anger pass, I pray thee for charity! And then by St. John, if thou may prove that I have done such a deed, let me be hanged on a tree! If any man hath wickedly lied about us, whatsoever he be, I will meet him in battle to make us quit and clear!"

Amis and Amiloun

"Yea," said the duke, "wilt thou so? Darest thou go into battle to make you both quit and free?"

"Yea, sir, verily," he said, "and thereto is my glove! He lied about us through enmity."

The steward started towards him, crying: "False traitor, thou shalt be attainted! I saw it myself this very day, how she was in thy chamber; and neither of you may deny it!"

Thus the steward went on, and ever Sir Amis said: "Nay, certainly, it was not so!"

Then the duke sent for his daughter, in that the steward was stubborn to avow the deed; and the maiden wept and wrung her hands and swore before her mother: "For certain it was not so!"

At last the duke said: "Without fail, it shall be proved in battle between those two knights."

Accordingly a combat was arranged betwixt them, and set for that day fortnight, where many men might see. And the steward was so powerful that in all the court was none willing to be surety for Sir Amis; but for the strong steward himself were soon found enough to borrow 12 him, twenty together. Thereupon they all said that Sir Amis must go to prison, being afraid that he might flee.

But the young maiden swore by Jesu Almighty that this were great wrong: "Take my body for that knight, and put me in a strong prison till his day of battle be come; and if he be fled and dare not uphold his right at that time, in undertaking the combat, do with me according to the law of the land, and let me for his sake be drawn, and hanged high on the gallows!"

And her mother said boldly that by the will of God she too would be his surety, that as a good knight he would maintain his day of battle and fight his foe. So those two fair ladies pledged their bodies for him; and the lords said every one that they would have none other borrows, but granted these.

When this was all done, and these sureties had been found and accepted, Sir Amis sorrowed day and night. All his joy was departed, and he was beset with care, in that the steward was so strong and had right on his side, while he himself was guilty of the charge against him.

He recked naught of his own life, but he thought so much of the maiden that no man might grieve more; for he remembered him that he must needs before the battle swear an oath that, as God should speed him, he was guiltless of the deed that was brought against him, and he thought that he had liefer be hanged than forsworn, and often he besought Jesus to save them both that they might not be doomed for ever.

So it befell on a day that he met the lady and her daughter by an orchard-side. "Sir Amis," the lady began, "why mournest thou so heavily? Tell me the truth. Dread thee naught in fighting with thy foe.

Whether thou ridest or goest afoot, I shall arm thee so well that thou need never fear to abide battle with him!"

"Madam," said the gentle knight, "for Jesus' sake, be not wroth! He hath the right and I the wrong, and therefore I am afeared to fight, God save me! For without fail, I must swear that, as God may speed me in the battle, his speech is false; and if I swear, I am forsworn, and I am lost, body and soul! Certes, I know no counsel!"

Then said that lady after a while: "Is there no other device to bring the traitor down?"

"Yes, dame," said he, "by St. Giles! There dwells hence, many a mile, my brother, Sir Amiloun; and if I durst go to him, I swear by St. John, he is so true that he would help me in this need, even at the cost of his own life, in battle with that felon!"

"Sir Amis," quoth the lady, "take leave to-morrow at daybreak, and wend on thy journey. I will say thou art gone home to thine own country to see thy father and mother; and when thou comest to thy brother, pray him as a noble knight of great goodness to undertake for us the battle against the steward that would wickedly destroy us all three."

On the morrow, Sir Amis busked him, took leave and fared forth on his journey, and spared not spur, pricking his horse, night and day without rest until, in a far country, the beast was overcome and fell down dead. Then was he helpless indeed, and his song became "Well-a-way!"

Amis and Amiloun

When this had befallen, he must needs go afoot, and, heavy-hearted, girt up his gown, and journeyed forth to keep his promise. All that day he ran until at twilight he came to a wild forest, when so strong a sleep overcame him that he could not have gone farther to win all the wealth of this world. He laid him under a tree and fell asleep, and lay still all that night till on the morrow men might see the day on both sides. 13 Now his brother, Sir Amiloun, was holden for a lord of great renown through all that countryside, and dwelled distant from the wood where Amis lay only half a day's journey, either to walk or ride. And as the gentle knight, Sir Amiloun, lay asleep on that same night, he dreamed that he saw Sir Amis, his sworn brother, belapped by his foes, by a raging wild bear and other beasts, all beset to death; and he stood alone among them, as a man that knew no remedy, in a woeful plight.

When Sir Amiloun awakened, he began to sorrow for him, and told his wife how he thought he saw black beasts thronging about his brother with hateful intent to slay him cruelly. "Certes," he said, "he is, through some wrong, in great peril, and stripped of all his joy; forsooth, I shall never rest content until I know how he fares!"

All at once he started up and would not linger, but busked him to ride forth, and when all his meiny geared them also, he bade them, for God's love, hold their peace, and swore by the Maker of mankind that none should go with him but himself alone.

Full richly he armed him and leaped upon his steed in haste, and bade all his men that none be so hardy as to follow him.

So through the night he rode until at daybreak he found Sir Amis up in that wide forest, whom at first he saw only as a wearied knight sleeping under a tree; so went to him and called: "Arise, fellow; it is light, and time for to go."

Sir Amis opened his eyes, and knew at once the gentle knight, his brother; and Sir Amiloun likewise perceived who it was, and dismounted, and they kissed each the other.

"Brother," said Amiloun, "why liest thou here thus mournful? Who hath wrought thee this woe?"

"Brother," answered Amis, "verily, I had never such sorrow sith I was born! For a while after thou didst leave me, I served my lord with much joy and bliss; but the steward, full

Amis and Amiloun

of envy, treachery and guile, hath brought me into such care that unless thou help me in this need, certes, there is no other way but that my life be lost!"

"Brother," said Sir Amiloun, "why hath the steward, that felon, done thee all this shame?"

"Certes," he answered, "with his treason he would bring me low; therefore hath he charged me!" Then he told all the case of himself and the maiden, and how the steward had betrayed them, and how the duke would have slain him, being fiercely enangered. And also he told how he had undertaken battle with the accuser, and how at court there was none who, to save those two bright ladies, durst stand as surety for himself, and how he must, without fail, swear ere he went into battle what would be a full strong lie: "And a man that is forsworn shall never speed! Certes, therefore, I know not what to do! ÔAlas' may well be my song!"

When Sir Amis had told all, how the false steward would bring him low, Sir Amiloun swore with bold words: "By Him that Judas sold, who died upon the Tree, he shall now fail of his hope; and I shall undertake battle for thee though he wax mad with rage! If ever I meet him, I shall see his heart's blood on my bright sword! But, brother," he said, "take all my weeds, and I shall put on thy robe, right as I were thyself. And I will swear, so may God speed me, as I am guiltless of that deed that he charged upon thee!"

Thereupon these noble knights changed their raiment, and when they were all yare, said Sir Amiloun: "By St. Giles, this man shall trip up the shrew that would ruin thee!"

"Brother," he said, "wend now to my home and my fair lady, and do as I bid thee. As thou art a gentle knight, thou shalt lie by her in bed till that I come again, and say thou hast sent thy steed to thy brother, Sir Amis. Then will they all be fain, as weening it is I. There is none that will know thee, so are we both alike."

When he had thus spoken, Sir Amiloun set out on his journey; and Sir Amis went anon to his brother's bright lady without more delay, and said how he had sent his steed as a rich gift to Sir Amis, by a knight of that country. And the folk supposed that Sir Amis was their own lord, so were they two alike; and when he had told his tale, all those at the court, little or great, less or more, thought it was true. When night came, Sir Amis and that fair lady went to bed; and when they were there together, Sir Amis drew his sword and laid it betwixt the two of them.

Amis and Amiloun

The lady looked upon him in anger, as thinking her lord were mad.

"Sir," she said, "why dost thou so? Thou wert not wont to do such a thing! Who hath changed thy mind?"

"Dame," he answered, "I have a malady that runs through my blood, and my bones are so sore that I would not come near thee for all this world's goods!"

Thus for a fortnight was that noble knight holden for a lord of high estate; but never once did he forget to lay his sword betwixt him and that bright lady. And she supposed, with all reason, that he was her husband, Sir Amiloun, that was sick; so she held her in peace and spoke no more words, but thought to await his will.

Now, gentles, hearken, and I will tell you how Sir Amiloun went on his way and spared not, but pricked his steed without cease, and came to court, stout and gay, the selfsame time that was appointed for the battle, and Sir Amis not there. The two ladies had been taken in hand to undergo their judgment with sorrow and heavy sighing. The steward waited upon a steed, with shield and spear, ready to offer fight, and began to blow out great boasts, and went before the duke anon, and said: "Sir, so God save me, hearken to my words. This traitor is gone forth from the land. If he were here, he should be hanged and drawn; therefore I ask for judgment that his sureties be burned, according to the law of the land!"

The duke, with wrathful intent, bade men should take the ladies and lead them forth; and a huge fire was made and a tun in which they might be burned. But thereupon folk looked across the field and saw a knight riding proudly with shield and spear, and they all said, "Yonder comes Sir Amis a-pricking," and prayed for delay.

Sir Amiloun stayed for no stone, but spurred among them all, and rode up to the duke. "My lord," he said anon, "for shame let these gracious, gentle ladies go free! I am come hither to-day to bring them out of their bonds and save them if I can; for certes, it were a great wrong so to roast bright ladies, and indeed a cruel thing!"

Then were the ladies so glad that they could tell no man their joy.

Amis and Amiloun

Their care was all vanished, and they went anon into the chamber and richly armed that knight with helmet and mail and bright byrnie. His attire was gay enough; and when he sat upon his horse, many a man prayed that day that God might save him and grant him victory.

As he went pricking out of the town, came a voice from heaven that none heard but he, and said: "Thou knight, Sir Amiloun, God that suffered the Passion hath sent thee a warning: if thou undertake this battle, thou shalt have a dread adventure within these three years; for ere they be passed, thou shalt be as foul a leper as ever was born in this world! But in that thou art so gentle and good, Jesus hath sent this message by me to give thee warning, that thou shalt be so foul a wretch with sorrow and care and poverty, as was never any man in worse estate! Over all this world, far and near, those that were thy best friends shall be thy greatest foes; and thy wife and thy kinsfolk shall flee the place where thou art, and forsake thee, one and all!"

The knight was still as a stone, as he hearkened to these cruel words; and he wist not what were best to do, to flee or to go into battle, and was sore troubled at heart. He thought: "If I make known who I am, then shall my brother be so put to shame that sorrow will bring him to his ending. Certes, for dread of punishment I must not fail to keep my word! God's will be done!"

All the folk that were there thought it was Sir Amis who offered battle. He and the steward were brought before the justice to take oath on that deed: the steward swore among the people that as truly as he had said no wrong, so might God help him in the fight; and Sir Amiloun swore that as truly as he had never kissed the maid, so might Our Lady speed him.

When they had taken their oaths, these barons were eager for the attack, and busked them to ride. All men, young and old alike, besought God to help Sir Amis at that time. They rode together on their stalwart steeds until their long spears met and splintered on each side; and then they drew their good swords and hewed together without cease.

Fiercely they fought with keen falchions; like madmen they dang each other's helmets with such strong, hard strokes that fire flew forth, and the blood spurted from grimly-wide wounds. From morning till noon lasted the battle between them in their furious mood.

Amis and Amiloun

Then Sir Amiloun sprang wrathfully at the other, as quick as fire from flint but his mighty stroke fell short and caught the steward's horse on the head and scattered his brains. When his steed fell dead on the ground, the steward feared lest he too should be slain; but Sir Amiloun dismounted, and went afoot to help him up. "Arise, steward," he said, "ye must fight on foot now ye have lost your horse; for it were great villainy, by St. John, to slay a man that lay fallen on the ground!"

He was a courteous knight, and took the steward by the hand, saying: "May God speed me, ye shall fight afoot, else were it a great shame!"

Anon the steward and that doughty man fought together with glittering bare swords; and they strove so hard with each other that all their armour ran with blood, and they spared not at all. The steward smote Amiloun a great wound on his shoulder, grimly enough; and through that wound after, as ye shall hear, was he found out, all sorrowful, when his trouble was come upon him. But then he was wild with rage when his swan-white armour ran with blood; and with a sharp falchion he smote at that other fiercely, as a doughty man, until the brand pierced from the shoulder blade into the breast and came out through the heart; and as the steward fell dying, Sir Amiloun struck off his head, and gave thanks to God for His grace.

All the lordings of every degree were full glad then, and raised the head on a spear and bore it away to the town. And thence folk issued forth to meet him in a seemly procession, and led him to the tower with joy and as much state as were he a prince of pride. And as they came into the palace, all weened that he was his brother.

"Sir Amis," said the duke, "here before all my lords I grant thee the merry maid Belisaunt. Thou hast bought her dear to-day with grim wounds; and therefore I render unto thee here and now my land and my daughter to hold for evermore!"

Full blithe and fain was the gentle knight, and thanked the duke with all his heart; and no man at court knew his name save the two ladies only. Soon they found leeches to search his wound and make him whole; and they were all glad and thanked God a thousand times that the steward was slain.

But on a day he busked him, and said that he would go home to his own country to tell all his friends how he had sped in the battle; and the duke granted him leave and offered him

Amis and Amiloun

a proud array of knights, but he answered, "Nay," and said that no man should go with him.

So he went forth alone, without knight or swain, and never rested till he came home where Sir Amis had awaited his return, day by day, up in the forest. When they met together, joyfully he told how he had slain the steward, and how Sir Amis should espouse the fair maiden. He dismounted, and they began to change their weeds as they had done before. "Brother," said he, "now mayst thou wend home again;" and he taught him what to say.

Then was Sir Amis glad and blithe, and thanked him a thousand times that ever he was born; and even until the moment that they should part a–two, he thanked him for his help and his good deed. "Brother,"

said he, "if it so betide that thou have ever care or woe, and are in need of my help, come or send thy messenger, and I shall never refuse thee—so God grant me grace! Be it of peril the sorest, I will help thee, wrong or right, even to the loss of my life!"

Thus they parted asunder, and Sir Amiloun returned home to his lady, and was full welcome to his friends. And at night when he went to bed and kissed his fair dame she asked him why he had been so strange all this fortnight, and laid his sword between them; and he bethought him then that his brother had been true. "Dame," he said, "I shall tell thee how it was, but look thou betray me to no man!"

She asked him then, for His love that won the world, to tell her what had befallen; and presently he told her all the case: how he had gone to court and how he had slain the steward, who with treason would have ruined his brother, and how it was Sir Amis, not himself, who had been there all that while.

The lady was very wroth, and often missaid her lord that night while they talked together: "With grievous wrong didst thou slay that gentle knight! Verily it was an ill deed!"

"Dame," he answered, "by Heaven's King, I did it only to save my brother from woe; and I hope, if I had need, he would help me as much, even to the risk of his life!"

Amis and Amiloun

Sir Amis rejoiced, as we tell in story, on his way to court; and when he came home he was honoured by all, earl and baron, knight and swain.

The duke took him by the hand, and seised him in all his possessions, to hold for ever; and afterwards, upon a day, he espoused Belisaunt, the true and kind.

Seemly were the folk gathered at that bridal; and there was held a royal feast of earls and barons and other lords with their bright ladies.

And over all that land, east and west, Sir Amis was accounted the flower of knighthood.

Within two years, Almighty God decreed that a fair grace should befall them. The duke died and his lady also, and they were buried in the cold earth; and Sir Amis was made duke over all that great land. And even more, as the story tells us, he had two children that were the fairest in the world.

While, then, he was lord of many a tower and town, and a duke all-powerful, his brother, Sir Amiloun, that was before so good and brave, was now all beaten down with heavy care; for, as the angel had foretold, he had become the foulest leper in the world. It is a pitiful thing to read in the story what sorrow he had, within two years, in return for his good deed! Ere the three years were ended, he wist not whither to turn, so heavy was his woe; for all that had been his best friends, and all his rich kinsmen, had now become his worst enemies, and his wife, to speak truth, treated him more cruelly, night and day, than did any of them.

When he was fallen into that hard case, a friendlesser man than he was might nowhere be found.

So wicked and shrewish was his lady that her hard and bitter words pierced his heart as with a knife, when she said to him: "Thou wretched caitiff, the steward was unjustly slain, as appears in thee; and therefore, by St. Denis of France, art thou fallen into this evil case! Curses on him that gives thee help!"

Oftentimes he wrung his hands as a man in such sorrow and distress that he finds his life all too long. Alas, alas, the gentle knight that was once both brave and of good counsel, was now brought so low that he was forbidden his own chamber at night, and in his own

Amis and Amiloun

hall was driven away from the high board and charged to sit at the table's end, where no man would be his neighbour. And when he had eaten thus in the hall for half a year, his lady waxed wroth and thought he lived too long: "Word has spread throughout this land that I feed a leper at my board, and be so foul a thing that it shames my kinsfolk; wherefore, by Jesus, Heaven's King, he shall sit by me no more!"

On a day, she called him and said: "Sir, it so happens that thou eatest too long in the hall. Forsooth, it is a great shame to all of us, and my kinsfolk are wroth with me!"

The knight wept, and said full low: "Put me where thou wilt, so no man see me. I pray of thee no more than a meal's meat each day, for St.

Charity!"

Anon that lady bade men to take timber, and half a mile from the gate to make a little lodging for her lord by the wayside. When it was finished, he would have nought of his gold save only the cup; and there alone in his lodge he made his moan to God in Heaven, and thanked Him for what He was pleased to send.

In all the court was no man to serve him when he went away to his lodge, save a gentle child called Owain, his sister's son, who wept for him bitterly, and said that he would never leave off to serve that knight, foot and hand, as long as he lived.

Now this fair, brave child came of gentle blood, and as soon as he was twelve years old he was called Amoraunt. Every night he slept by his lord, and every day he fetched the day's food whereon they lived; and while other men sang and made merry, he was ever sorrowful for his lord's sake, Each day, as I have told you, he came to court, and stinted for no strife. When they all told him to forsake that beggar that he might the better speed, he answered them courteously, but swore by Him that died on the Rood and suffered wounds five, that he would never forsake his lord while he lived—not for all this world's goods! When a twelvemonth had passed, and Amoraunt still went to fetch his lord's livery, the lady became wroth and bade her men drive the child away, and swore by Him that Judas sold, though his lord died of hunger and cold where he lay, he should have nor meat nor drink, nor any other help from her after that.

Amis and Amiloun

The child wrung his hands, and went home weeping and sighing bitterly. When the good man bade him tell why it was, he answered and said: "Verily, no wonder though I be woe! My heart breaks for care! Thy wife hath sworn in great anger that she will help us no more! Alas, what shall we do?"

"God help us!" quoth that gentle knight. "Whilom I was a great man, able to deal out food and clothing; and now I am so foul that all who look upon me loathe that sight. Son," he said, let be thy weeping, although this is bitter news, forsooth Certes, I know none other counsel but we must beg our bread. Now I wot well how it goes!"

On the morrow at daybreak, the child and the gentle knight made them ready to go forth and beg their bread, as they had need to do, for they had no food. They wandered up and down the roads until they came to a market-town five miles away; and, bitterly weeping, from door to door they begged their food, for the love of God. 24 At that time there was great plenty in the land alike of meat and drink; and folk were free of giving, and put into their hands enough of all kinds of things. And because the good man was so unfortunate and the child so fair, old and young loved them and brought them so much of goods that Amoraunt was blithe and left off his weeping.

At last the good man grew footsore, so that he might not go farther for all the wealth of this world; and thereupon the child bore him to the town's end, and built him a lodging where folk passed on their way to market. And the country-people who went every day to their cheaping 25 gave them food; but often, as well, Amoraunt went into the town and begged meat and drink, when their need was greatest.

Thus, as we read in the story, they dwelled there for three years, the child and he; and lived in poverty and care among the country-folk, as they went to and fro. But, in the fourth year, corn waxed so dear that neither old nor young would give them meat or drink; and they were in great distress.

Amoraunt went often into the town, but could not get food from man or woman; and when they were alone together, they moaned with rueful lamentation that they were still alive. And all the while his lady lived thence not five miles, and made merry night and day while he lay in such sorrow—curses upon her! On a day as they sat there alone, that good knight said mournfully to the child: "Son, thou must go to my lady, who dwells hard by; and pray her by Him that died on the Rood, to send me of my own goods an ass to ride upon, and then will we go forth from this land to beg our bread, nor abide here longer."

Amoraunt went to the court before that noble lady, and said to her in courteous wise: "Madam, verily my lord hath sent me as a messenger, because he himself cannot walk, and prays you humbly to grant him of his goods an ass to ride upon; and we shall go forth from the land and never come here again though hunger slay us!"

The lady said she would fain send him two asses if only he would go away so far that he might never come again.

"Nay, certes, dame," said the child, "ye shall never see us more!"

Thereupon she was glad, and commanded an ass to be given him, and said sternly: "Now ye shall fare forth from the land, and God grant that ye come here never again!"

The child waited no longer, but bestrode his ass, and went home and told his lord how shamefully his lady had spoken at that time. He set the knight upon the good beast, and they were full fain to go forth from the city. Up and down through many a country they wandered, begging their meat from town to town, alike in wind and rain.

But over all that land, by God's will, there passed so fierce a famine, as far as they went, that they near died of hunger, and had not half their fill of bread. They were so woeful that on a day the knight spake: "Behoves us sell our ass, for we have no other goods save my rich golden cup; but, certes, that shall never be sold, though I perish of hunger!"

Then early one morning, Sir Amiloun and Amoraunt with heavy sorrow went to a market–town; and when the knight had dismounted, Amoraunt went anon into the city, leading the ass, and sold it for five shillings. And while the famine was so great that they might get nothing, they bought therewith their food.

After the ass was sold for five shillings, as I have said, they dwelled there three days until Amoraunt waxed strong again, being now of fifteen winters and right courteous and noble. He grieved for his lord, and took him on his back and bore him out of that city; and for half a year and somewhat more, he carried him about to beg his food blessings on the child! Thus he did until the long, hard winter came on, when "Alas!" was often his song, so was that country deep [in mud]. The roads were so bemired and sliddery that often they both fell down together in the clay. And still was Amoraunt true and kind by nature and served his lord as best he might, and would not leave him. And so as he carried him about on his back, serving him day and night, his song was often "Well-a-way;" and for the deep mud of that country his bones were full sore. By that time all their money was spent save twelve pence, wherewith they went and bought a good push-cart; and the child placed his lord therein, for he might carry him no longer.

And after, Amoraunt pushed Sir Amiloun back and forth through many a country, until he came to a city-town where the bold Sir Amis was duke and lord of all the land. Then said the knight: "Try to bring me as far as the duke's court hard by. He is a mild man, and by God's grace, we shall there get something. But, dear son, for His love that won the world, as thou art true and good, tell no man whither I go or whence I come, or what my name is."

He answered, "Nay," and went to court; and before all the other poor men there he pushed his cart in the fen, as was a pity to see.

It befell that same day, as I tell you with tongue, that it was midwinter-tide. The great duke came proudly home from church, and when he entered the castle gate, the poor men drew a little aside, as with knights and many serjeants he went into his seemly hall, there to rest with great mirth and revelry.

As it is the law of kings' courts, the trumpets blew for men to go to meat, and when they were all set a-row, they were served full merrily.

And while the duke drank from gold cups, he that had brought him to be in such worship stood shut out at the gate, sorely an-hungered and cold.

It happened that a knight and a serjeant went outside the castle to disport them together; and by the grace of God they caught sight of Sir Amiloun, who was so loathly to look upon, and after, of Amoraunt, who was so gentle of bearing that they both said, in all the court was none half his peer in goodliness.

Now this worthy knight went up to him and courteously asked him from what land he came, and why he stood there, and whom he served.

Amis and Amiloun

"Sir," he answered, "God save me, I am my lord's knave that lieth here in bonds. If thou art a knight of gentle blood, bear our errand to some good ending, for God's sake!"

Anon the good man asked him if he would leave that beggar and serve himself; and he said further that, by St. John, he should be at the court of that great duke, who would make him a rich man.

But he answered and swore by Him who died on the Rood, that as long as he might walk, he would not forsake his lord—not to win all this world's wealth.

Then the good man believed him either mad, or else a silly fool that had lost his wits; or else, he thought, the foul-visaged man must be of high rank. So he spoke no more with them, but went back into the hall before the great duke, and said: "My lord, listen to me; it is the finest jest, by my faith, that ever thou hast heard since thou wert born!"

Thereupon the duke bade him tell it before them all without delay.

"Now, sir," he said, "by St. John, I was outside the gate right now for my disport, and I saw many poor men there, old and young, and among them a beggar who is the foulest thing ever heard of in any land. He lies in a wain, so feeble of strength that he may not go afoot, and by him stood a youth, almost naked, who is the gentlest child on earth, and the fairest to whom Christ ever gave life or christening; but he is the greatest fool, verily, in all this world!"

Then the duke asked: "What folly saith he? Is he mad?"

"Sir," he answered, I prayed him to forsake the beggar in the wain that he stood by, and come into your service, and I promised him land and fee, worldly goods enough; but he answered and said that he would never go from him; therefore, I hold him mad."

Then said the duke: "Though his lord be in such evil state, peradventure the good man hath before holpen him in time of need, or the child is of his kin, or hath sworn oaths never to forsake him. Whether he be a stranger or of his blood," he said, "it is a good child and true, God speed me! If I speak with him ere he depart, I shall reward him for being so faithful and so kind!"

Amis and Amiloun

Anon the duke called to him a bold squire, and said: "Take my golden cup as full of wine as thou mayst hold it with thy two hands, and carry it to the castle gate, where thou shalt find a beggar lying in a wain, and bid him and his page to drink this wine, and then bring me back the cup."

The squire received it, and to the castle gate bore it full of wine, and said to the leper: "My lord hath sent thee this cup of wine; drink it if thou dare!"

Then the beggar drew forth his own golden cup as like that other as had it been the same, for they were cast in one mould; and when he had poured in the wine there was no difference between them.

The squire as he stood there gazed at the two cups, first the beggar's and then his lord's; but he could not choose which was the better of them so were they alike. He ran again into the hall, and said: "Certes, sir, thou hast wasted many a good deed, and even this now! He is a richer man than thou art, by the day when God was born!"

"Nay," answered the duke, "that could not be; it were against the law!"

"Yes, sir," he said, "he is a traitor, by my fay, and worthy to be drawn; for when I took him the wine, he drew forth a fine gold cup, right as it were thine own. In all this world, by St. John, there is no man so wise as to know them apart!"

"Now, certes," quoth Sir Amis, "there were never cups so alike in all ways, save mine and my brother's, that we had in token of our parting.

And if it be the same, then my dear brother, Sir Amiloun, is dead through treason; and if this beggar hath stolen his cup, I will slay him myself to day, by Jesu, Heaven's King!"

He started up from the table, and seized his sword like a madman, and drew it from its sheath, and ran to the castle gate; and no man in all the court dared to stop him. He rushed upon the beggar in his wain and seized him with his two hands and slung him into the lake, and laid strokes upon him so madly that all who stood about had great pity.

"Traitor!" cried the bold duke. "Whence hadst thou this golden cup? How camest thou thereto? For by Him that Judas sold, it belonged to my brother Amiloun when he went

Amis and Amiloun

away from me!"

"Yea, certes, sir," began that other, "it was his in his country; but now things have so fallen out that it is mine, and bought dear. I came by it by right!"

Then was the duke so wild of mood that none who stood about him durst lay hands on him. He spurned the beggar with his foot and laid on him furiously with his naked sword; and drew him by the feet and trod him in the mud without cease, crying: "Thief, thou shalt be slain! But first thou shalt make known the truth, whence thou hadst the cup!"

Child Amoraunt stood in the throng, and saw how unjustly and woefully his lord was abused; and being himself hardy and strong, he caught the duke in his arms and held him still. "Sir," he cried, "ye are cruel and unjust to slay that gentle knight! Bitterly may he rue the time that ever he undertook battle to save your life! He is your brother Amiloun, once a noble baron, but now thus beaten down by affliction! May God who suffered the Passion bring him out of his woe! For your sake is he robbed of all bliss, and ye repay him by breaking his bones a–two! Well ye reward him for helping you in your need! Alas, why fare ye so?"

When Sir Amis heard this, he ran straight to the knight and took him in his two arms, and often cried, "Alas!" and made his song, "Wellaway!"

He looked at the leper's bare shoulder, and perceived by the grim wound thereon that it was all as Amoraunt said; and then he fell a–swooning, and cried "Alack the while"—that ever he had lived to see that day. "Alas," he said, "my joy is departed! Never was man more cruel! I know not what to do! For saving my life of yore, I have repaid him with sorrow and scorn, and have wrought him much woe! O brother, par charit", forgive me this rueful deed, that I have so smitten thee!"

And Amiloun forgave him at once, and often kissed him, weeping.

Then Sir Amis also wept for joy, and lifted his brother in his two arms, and would not let any other man bear him until he came into the hall.

There stood his lady and deemed her lord mad, and ran to meet him, crying: "Sir, what is thy thought? Why hast thou brought this man into the hall, by Him that won the world?"

Amis and Amiloun

"O dame," he said, "by St. John, never have I been so sorrowful, if thou wouldst know the truth; for there is no better knight in the world than this, and I have nearhand slain him, and shamefully maltreated! It is my noble brother Amiloun, who is so beaten down with sorrow and care!"

The lady wrung her hands and cried, "Alack the while!" and swooned away.

As foul a leper as he was, she kissed him there and spared not; and often she cried, "Alas!"—that on him was fallen such a hard chance, to live always in sorrow and pain. She led him into her chamber, and cast aside all his poor garments and bathed his body, and brought him soon to a bed that was furnished with rich coverings.

They were full fain to have him there, and were true and kind to him as he lay a twelvemonth in their chamber; nor would they deny him aught that he asked for, night or day. He lacked nothing of the meat and drink that they themselves had, so dealt they both with him gently; and as the twelvemonth drew to its end, a fair grace alighted on them all, as ye shall hear.

It befell one night, as Sir Amis lay asleep, that he thought a bright angel from heaven stood before his bed, and said to him that if he would arise on Christmas morning, such time as Jesus was born, and slay his two children, and with the blood anoint his brother, by God's grace Amiloun's sickness would be taken away. Thus for three nights he thought an angel warned him that if he would do this thing, his brother would be as fair a man as ever he was before.

At this Sir Amis was glad, but yet he was sorrowful for his two children, the fairest in the world. He was well loth to slay them, but well more loth to lose his kind brother, Amiloun.

That same night, Sir Amiloun dreamed that an angel warned him and said that if Amis would slay his children, their heart's-blood might take away his sickness.

On the morrow, Sir Amis went to his brother and asked him how he fared; and he answered in a low voice: "Brother, I abide here God's will, for I may do no more!"

Amis and Amiloun

As they sat there, talking of one thing and another, Sir Amiloun said presently: "Brother, I must needs tell thee in secret that to-night I dreamed of an angel come from heaven, who told me that by the blood of thy two children, I might escape from my sickness and be hale and whole!"

Then the duke remembered that to slay his young children were a deadly sin; and yet he thought that, by Heaven's King, he would not stop for that, to bring his brother out of pain.

So it befell on Christmas Eve when Jesu was born to save mankind, that the castle-folk dight them joyfully to go to church. When they were ready, the duke bade them, as they would be his friends, that all should go, and none remain in the chamber; and he said that he himself, for that night, would take care of his brother. And there was none durst gainsay him; so they all went to church and left only the two together.

But before they went to church, the duke had watched to see where the keys of the nursery were put, and slily he noted where they were; and when all were gone and he was left alone, he took a burning candle and found the keys, and went to the chamber where his children were.

And when he beheld how fair they lay and slept together, he said to himself: "By St. John, it were great pity to slay you whom God hath bought so dear!" He had already drawn his knife, but now for sorrow he slunk away aside, and wept bitterly.

But afterwards he turned his thought again, and said: "My brother was so good and kind that on a day he shed his blood for love of me through a grimly wound. Why now should I spare my children to bring him out of suffering? O certes," he said, "nay! To help my brother in his distress, God speed me, and Mary, that sweet Maid!"

He waited no longer, but heavy of heart, caught up his knife and seized his children, and—not to waste their blood—cut their throats over a basin. And when he had so done, he laid them in bed again—no wonder if he were woe!—and covered them so that it did not appear that any man had been with them; and so he left the chamber.

As he went out he steked the door as fast as it was erst, and hid the keys under a stone, and thought that folk would suppose them to be lost.

Amis and Amiloun

Then he went to his brother and said to that sorrowful man, at the very time when God was born: "I have brought thee my children's blood; and I hope it may heal thee as the angel hath said!"

"Brother," cried Amiloun, "hast thou slain thy two children? Alas, why didst thou so?" He wept and said, "Well−a−way! I had liefer have lived in care and sorrow till Doomsday!"

Then said Sir Amis: "Be still! Jesu may, when it is His will, send me more children. For my sake thou art now bare of bliss, and verily I will not spare my life to help thee out of thy pain!"

He took the blood, and therewith anointed the gentle knight, who once had been so fair; and after, he put him to bed and wrapped him warmly with many rich coverings.

"Now brother," he said, "lie still, and fall asleep, i' God's name; and as the angel said, I hope well that Jesu, Heaven's King, will heal thee of thy sickness!"

There Sir Amis left him and went into the chapel, as the story tells, and there made moan to God in Heaven for his children that he had slain; and he prayed with rueful cheer that He and His Mother Mary would save him from shame that day. And Jesus Christ in that place heard the knight's prayer and granted it.

On the morrow at daybreak, the lady came home full happily, with her knights fifteen; but when they had sought the keys and found them not, their joy was turned to care.

The duke bade them all to cease and to stint their strife; and he said that he had taken the keys, and no man should go into the chamber but himself and his duchess. He took his lady anon, and said to her: "Sweetheart, keep thee glad of heart! By Him that won this world, I have slain my dear children, for methought an angel came from heaven to me in my sleep, and told me that through their blood my brother should pass out of his affliction! Therefore I slew them both to heal that good man!"

Then was the lady ferly woe, but she saw that her lord was also in heavy grief, and began to comfort him: "O dear life, God may send us more children—cease to mourn for these! If it lay at my heart's root to bring thy brother help, I would not spare to die! No man shall see our children, and to-morrow they shall be buried right as they were dead in the course of nature!"

So this fair lady comforted her lord as best she might and after, they went both to Sir Amiloun and found that he was awake; and by God's grace all his foulness was gone, and he was once more as fair a man as ever he had been sith he was born.

Then were they all so blithe that they might not tell their joy, and gave thanks to God; and presently they went to the chamber where the children lay, and found them whole and sound, without hurt, and playing together in bed. They wept for joy as they stood there, and thanked God that he had taken all their care away.

By the time that Sir Amiloun was well and strong enough to walk and ride, Amoraunt was a bold squire and blithe of cheer to serve his lord.

And on a day, the knight said that he would go home to his own country and speak with his wife, and requite her for all the help that she had given him in time of need.

Then Sir Amis sent hastily for many good knights, five hundred keen and true; and, with other barons on palfrey and steed, Sir Amiloun pricked night and day until he came to his own country, and there found that one of his own knights had espoused his wife.

But it happened that he came home the very day the bridal was held; and pricked at once to the gates, where he began a sorry game among the bold barons. He sent a messenger into the hall to say that their lord was come home, the merriest man on earth; and thereupon the lady turned pale, and many a man, young and old, was heavy of cheer.

Sir Amis and Sir Amiloun, and all their stout barons, knights, and squires, in their helmets and habergeons, went into the hall with bright swords and brown; and they gave great strokes to all that they might reach, alike great and small. Glad were those that escaped that day, and fled from the bridal. When in their vengeance they had driven all men, brown and black, out of that noble hall, Sir Amiloun had built for his lady a great tower of lime and stone. Therein she was brought, and kept on bread and water till her life-days were done. And when she died, he that was sorry could have been naught but a villain, as ye may judge who have heard, one and all.

Amis and Amiloun

Then Sir Amiloun sent a messenger to earls and barons, free and bond; and when they had assembled, he seised Child Owain, who had been so true and kind, in all his lands. And when he had so done, he returned again with his brother, Sir Amis; and they led their lives together with much joy and without strife until God summoned them.

But first these two noble barons let build a fair abbey, and endowed it well in the land of Lombardy, that masses might be sung for themselves and their forefathers until Doomsday.

They both died on the same day, and were laid in one grave; and for their truth and goodness they have as meed the bliss of Heaven that lasteth evermore.

Amen.

Printed in the United States
25034LVS00002B/282